DATE DUE

GAYLORD   #3522PI   Printed in USA

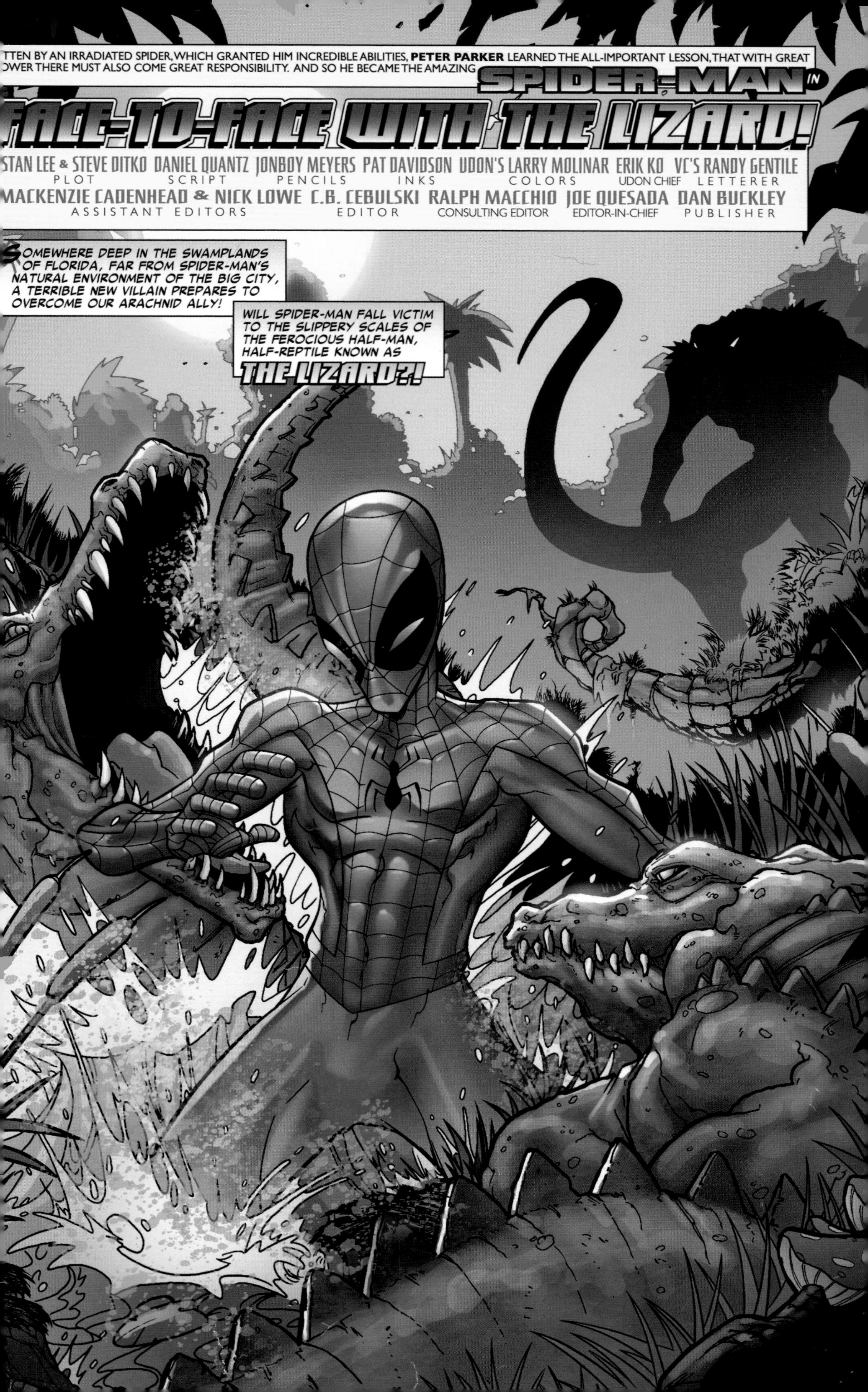

TTEN BY AN IRRADIATED SPIDER, WHICH GRANTED HIM INCREDIBLE ABILITIES, PETER PARKER LEARNED THE ALL-IMPORTANT LESSON, THAT WITH GREAT
OWER THERE MUST ALSO COME GREAT RESPONSIBILITY. AND SO HE BECAME THE AMAZING
SPIDER-MAN IN
FACE-TO-FACE WITH THE LIZARD!
STAN LEE & STEVE DITKO PLOT
DANIEL QUANTZ SCRIPT
JONBOY MEYERS PENCILS
PAT DAVIDSON INKS
UDON'S LARRY MOLINAR COLORS
ERIK KO UDON CHIEF
VC'S RANDY GENTILE LETTERER
MACKENZIE CADENHEAD & NICK LOWE ASSISTANT EDITORS
C.B. CEBULSKI EDITOR
RALPH MACCHIO CONSULTING EDITOR
JOE QUESADA EDITOR-IN-CHIEF
DAN BUCKLEY PUBLISHER
SOMEWHERE DEEP IN THE SWAMPLANDS OF FLORIDA, FAR FROM SPIDER-MAN'S NATURAL ENVIRONMENT OF THE BIG CITY, A TERRIBLE NEW VILLAIN PREPARES TO OVERCOME OUR ARACHNID ALLY!
WILL SPIDER-MAN FALL VICTIM TO THE SLIPPERY SCALES OF THE FEROCIOUS HALF-MAN, HALF-REPTILE KNOWN AS
THE LIZARD?!

VISIT US AT

www.abdopub.com

Spotlight, a division of ABDO Publishing Company Inc., is the school and library distributor of the Marvel Entertainment books.

Library bound edition © 2006

Library of Congress Cataloging-in-Publication Data

Face-to-Face With the Lizard!

ISBN 1-59961-014-0 (Reinforced Library Bound Edition)

All Spotlight books are reinforced library binding
and manufactured in the United States of America

Spotlight

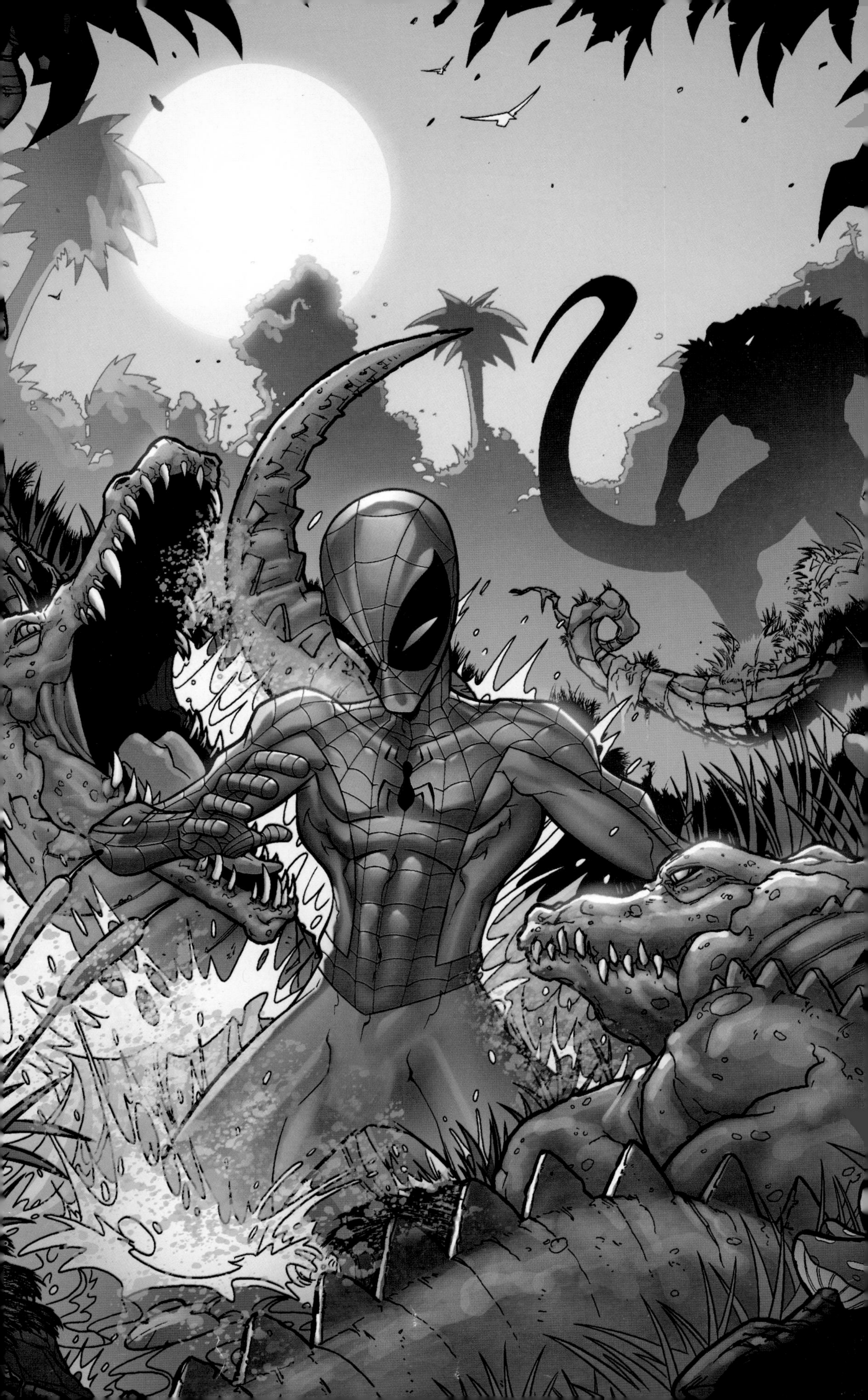

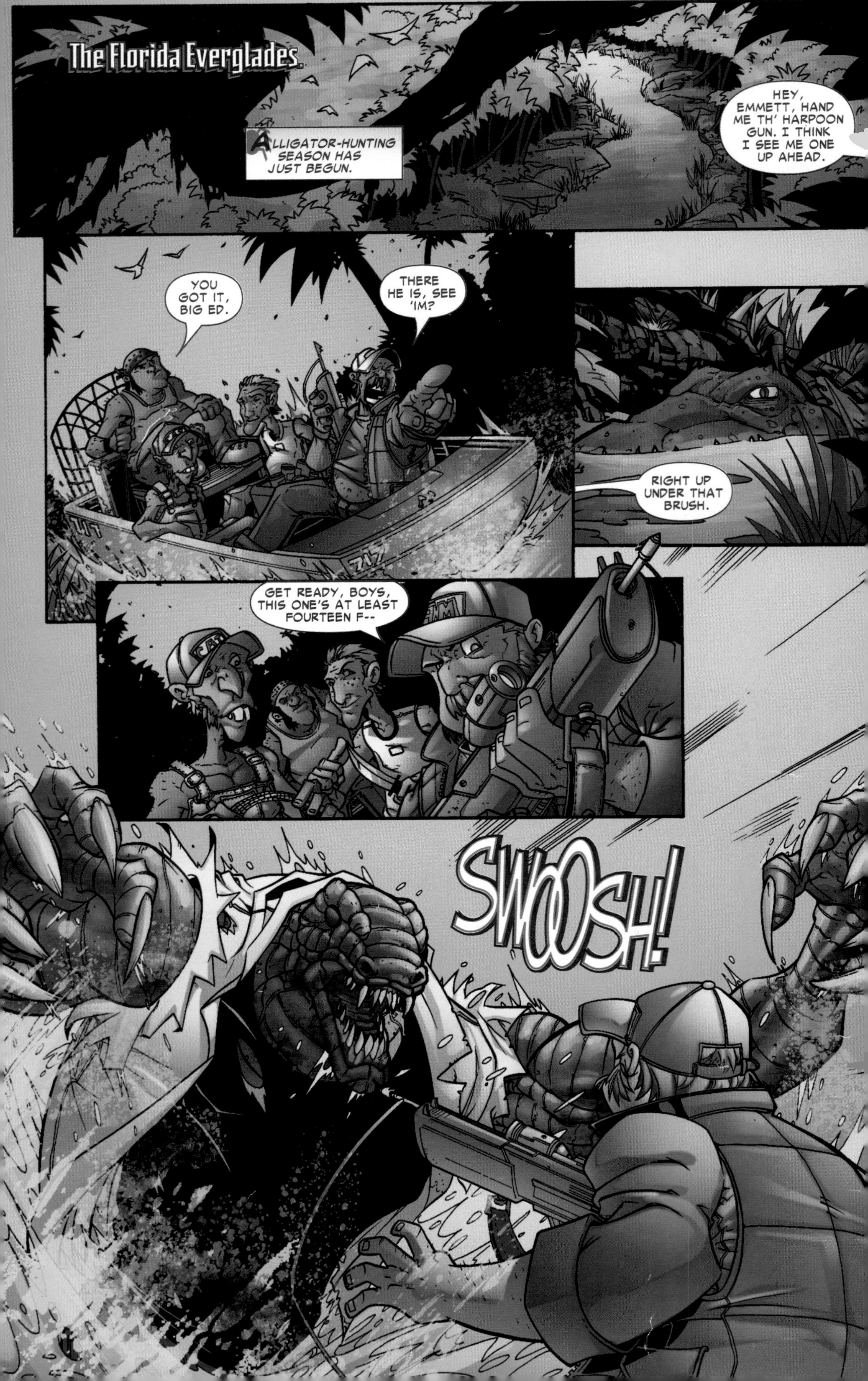
The Florida Everglades.
ALLIGATOR-HUNTING SEASON HAS JUST BEGUN.
HEY, EMMETT, HAND ME TH' HARPOON GUN. I THINK I SEE ME ONE UP AHEAD.
YOU GOT IT, BIG ED.
THERE HE IS, SEE 'IM?
RIGHT UP UNDER THAT BRUSH.
GET READY, BOYS, THIS ONE'S AT LEAST FOURTEEN F--
SWOOSH!

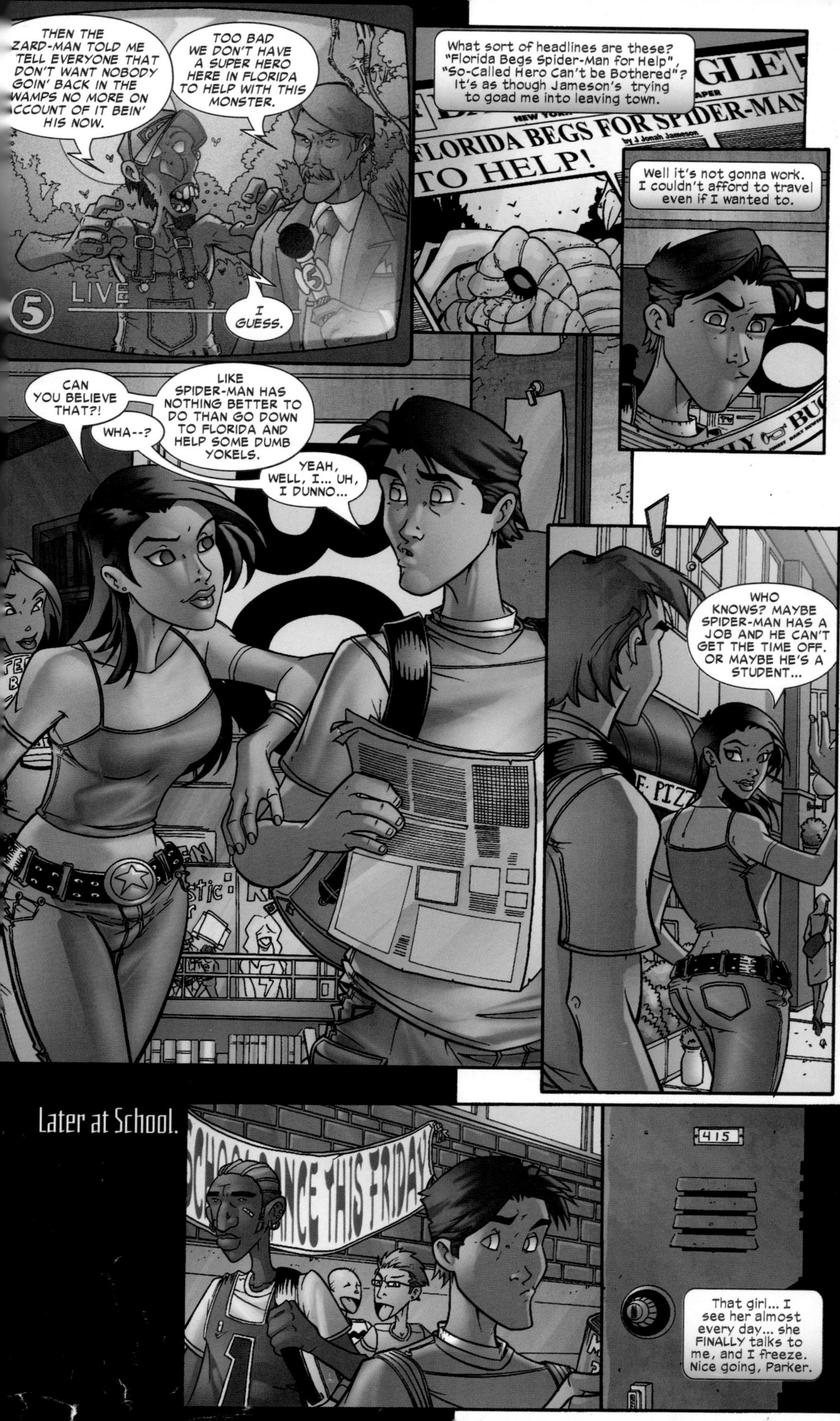
THEN THE ZARD-MAN TOLD ME TELL EVERYONE THAT DON'T WANT NOBODY GOIN' BACK IN THE WAMPS NO MORE ON CCOUNT OF IT BEIN' HIS NOW.
TOO BAD WE DON'T HAVE A SUPER HERO HERE IN FLORIDA TO HELP WITH THIS MONSTER.
LIVE
I GUESS.
What sort of headlines are these? "Florida Begs Spider-Man for Help", "So-Called Hero Can't be Bothered"? It's as though Jameson's trying to goad me into leaving town.
FLORIDA BEGS FOR SPIDER-MAN TO HELP!
by J Jonah Jameson
Well it's not gonna work. I couldn't afford to travel even if I wanted to.
CAN YOU BELIEVE THAT?!
LIKE SPIDER-MAN HAS NOTHING BETTER TO DO THAN GO DOWN TO FLORIDA AND HELP SOME DUMB YOKELS.
WHA--?
YEAH, WELL, I... UH, I DUNNO...
WHO KNOWS? MAYBE SPIDER-MAN HAS A JOB AND HE CAN'T GET THE TIME OFF. OR MAYBE HE'S A STUDENT...
Later at School.
415
That girl... I see her almost every day... she FINALLY talks to me, and I freeze. Nice going, Parker.

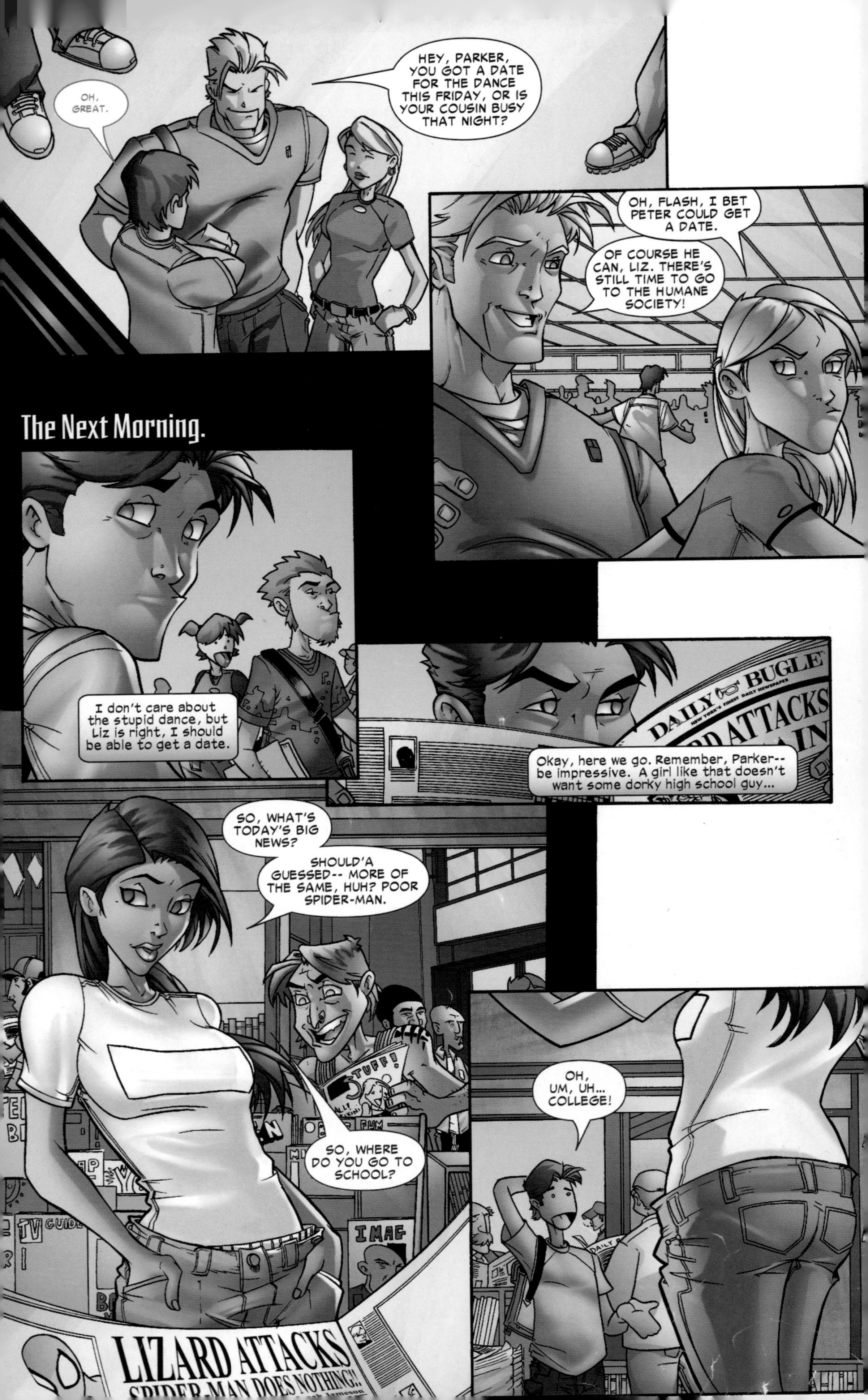

OH, GREAT.
HEY, PARKER, YOU GOT A DATE FOR THE DANCE THIS FRIDAY, OR IS YOUR COUSIN BUSY THAT NIGHT?
OH, FLASH, I BET PETER COULD GET A DATE.
OF COURSE HE CAN, LIZ. THERE'S STILL TIME TO GO TO THE HUMANE SOCIETY!
The Next Morning.
I don't care about the stupid dance, but Liz is right, I should be able to get a date.
DAILY BUGLE
Okay, here we go. Remember, Parker-- be impressive. A girl like that doesn't want some dorky high school guy...
SO, WHAT'S TODAY'S BIG NEWS?
SHOULD'A GUESSED-- MORE OF THE SAME, HUH? POOR SPIDER-MAN.
SO, WHERE DO YOU GO TO SCHOOL?
OH, UM, UH... COLLEGE!
LIZARD ATTACKS
SPIDER-MAN DOES NOTHING!!

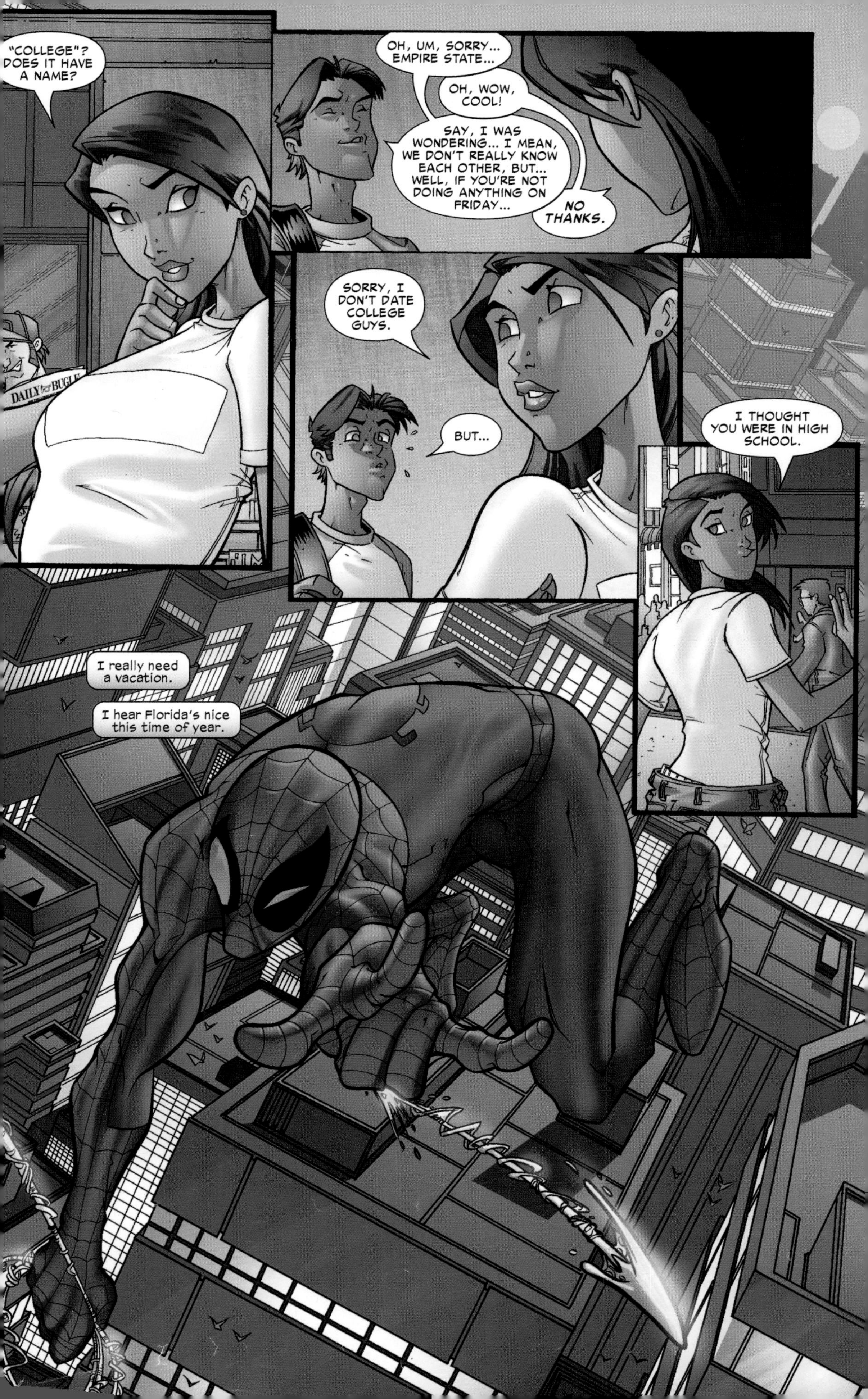
"COLLEGE"? DOES IT HAVE A NAME?
OH, UM, SORRY... EMPIRE STATE...
OH, WOW, COOL!
SAY, I WAS WONDERING... I MEAN, WE DON'T REALLY KNOW EACH OTHER, BUT... WELL, IF YOU'RE NOT DOING ANYTHING ON FRIDAY...
NO THANKS.
SORRY, I DON'T DATE COLLEGE GUYS.
BUT...
I THOUGHT YOU WERE IN HIGH SCHOOL.
I really need a vacation.
I hear Florida's nice this time of year.

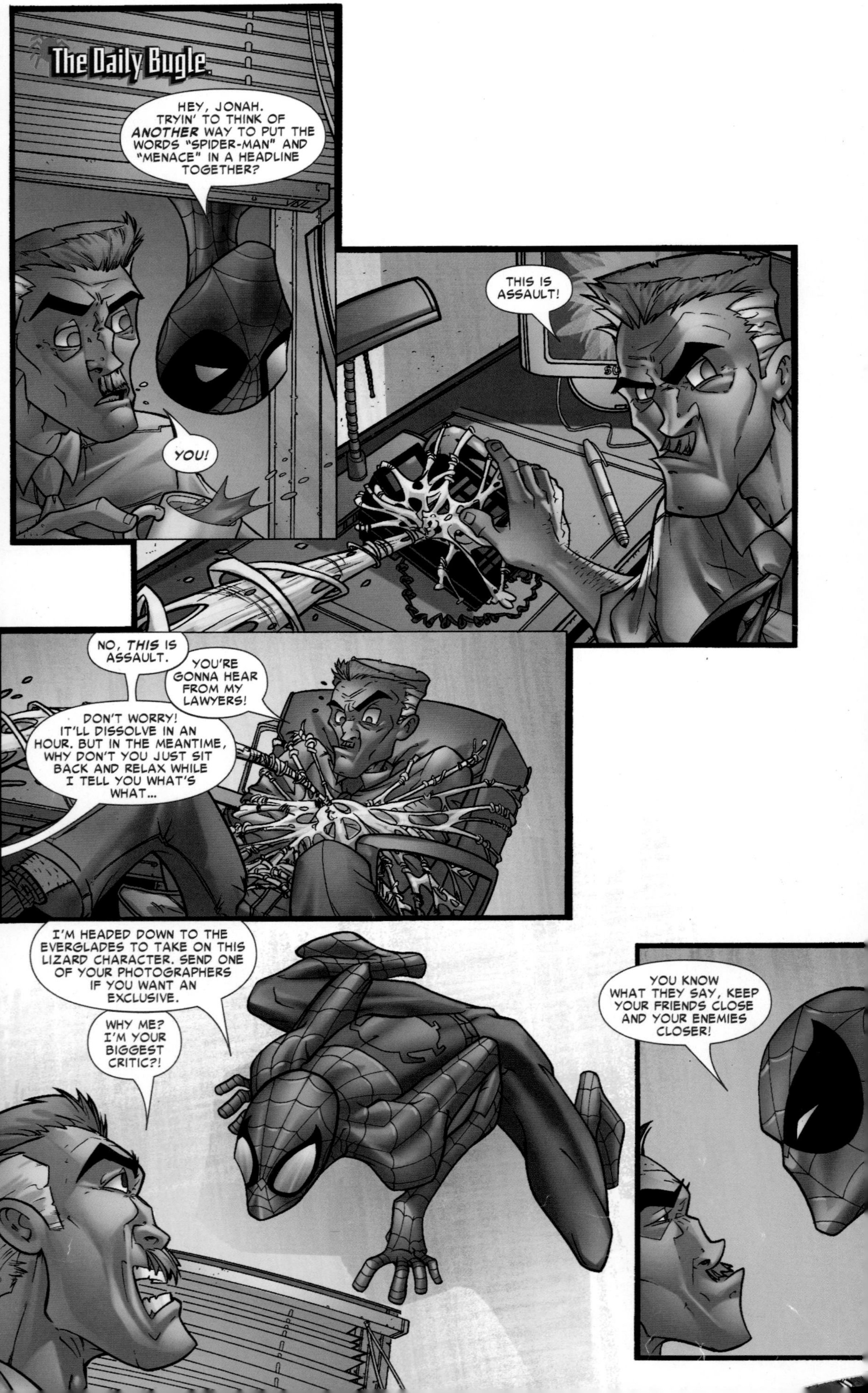
The Daily Bugle.
HEY, JONAH. TRYIN' TO THINK OF *ANOTHER* WAY TO PUT THE WORDS "SPIDER-MAN" AND "MENACE" IN A HEADLINE TOGETHER?
YOU!
THIS IS ASSAULT!
NO, *THIS* IS ASSAULT.
YOU'RE GONNA HEAR FROM MY LAWYERS!
DON'T WORRY! IT'LL DISSOLVE IN AN HOUR. BUT IN THE MEANTIME, WHY DON'T YOU JUST SIT BACK AND RELAX WHILE I TELL YOU WHAT'S WHAT...
I'M HEADED DOWN TO THE EVERGLADES TO TAKE ON THIS LIZARD CHARACTER. SEND ONE OF YOUR PHOTOGRAPHERS IF YOU WANT AN EXCLUSIVE.
WHY ME? I'M YOUR BIGGEST CRITIC?!
YOU KNOW WHAT THEY SAY, KEEP YOUR FRIENDS CLOSE AND YOUR ENEMIES CLOSER!

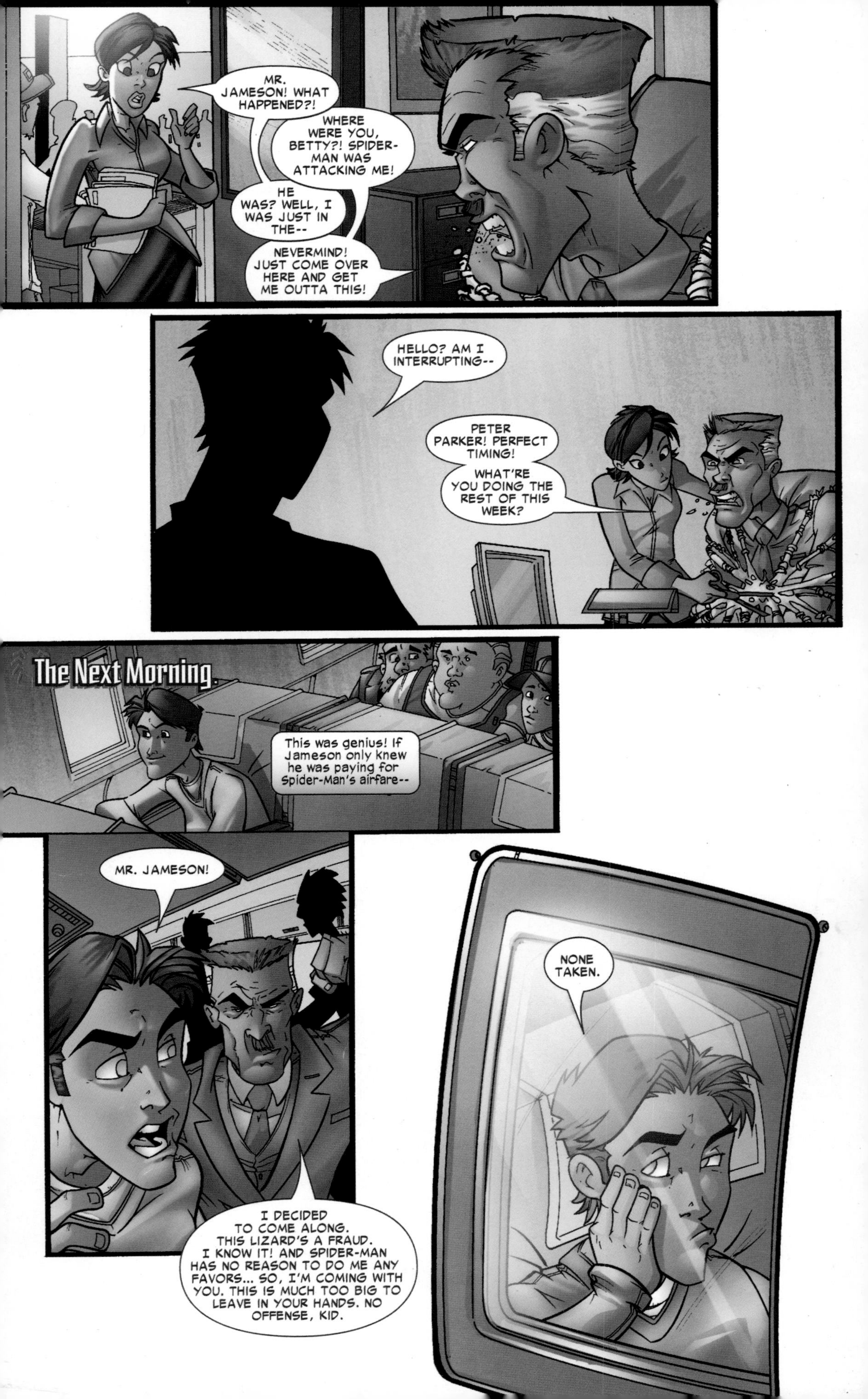
MR. JAMESON! WHAT HAPPENED?!
WHERE WERE YOU, BETTY?! SPIDER-MAN WAS ATTACKING ME!
HE WAS? WELL, I WAS JUST IN THE--
NEVERMIND! JUST COME OVER HERE AND GET ME OUTTA THIS!
HELLO? AM I INTERRUPTING--
PETER PARKER! PERFECT TIMING!
WHAT'RE YOU DOING THE REST OF THIS WEEK?
The Next Morning.
This was genius! If Jameson only knew he was paying for Spider-Man's airfare--
MR. JAMESON!
I DECIDED TO COME ALONG. THIS LIZARD'S A FRAUD. I KNOW IT! AND SPIDER-MAN HAS NO REASON TO DO ME ANY FAVORS... SO, I'M COMING WITH YOU. THIS IS MUCH TOO BIG TO LEAVE IN YOUR HANDS. NO OFFENSE, KID.
NONE TAKEN.

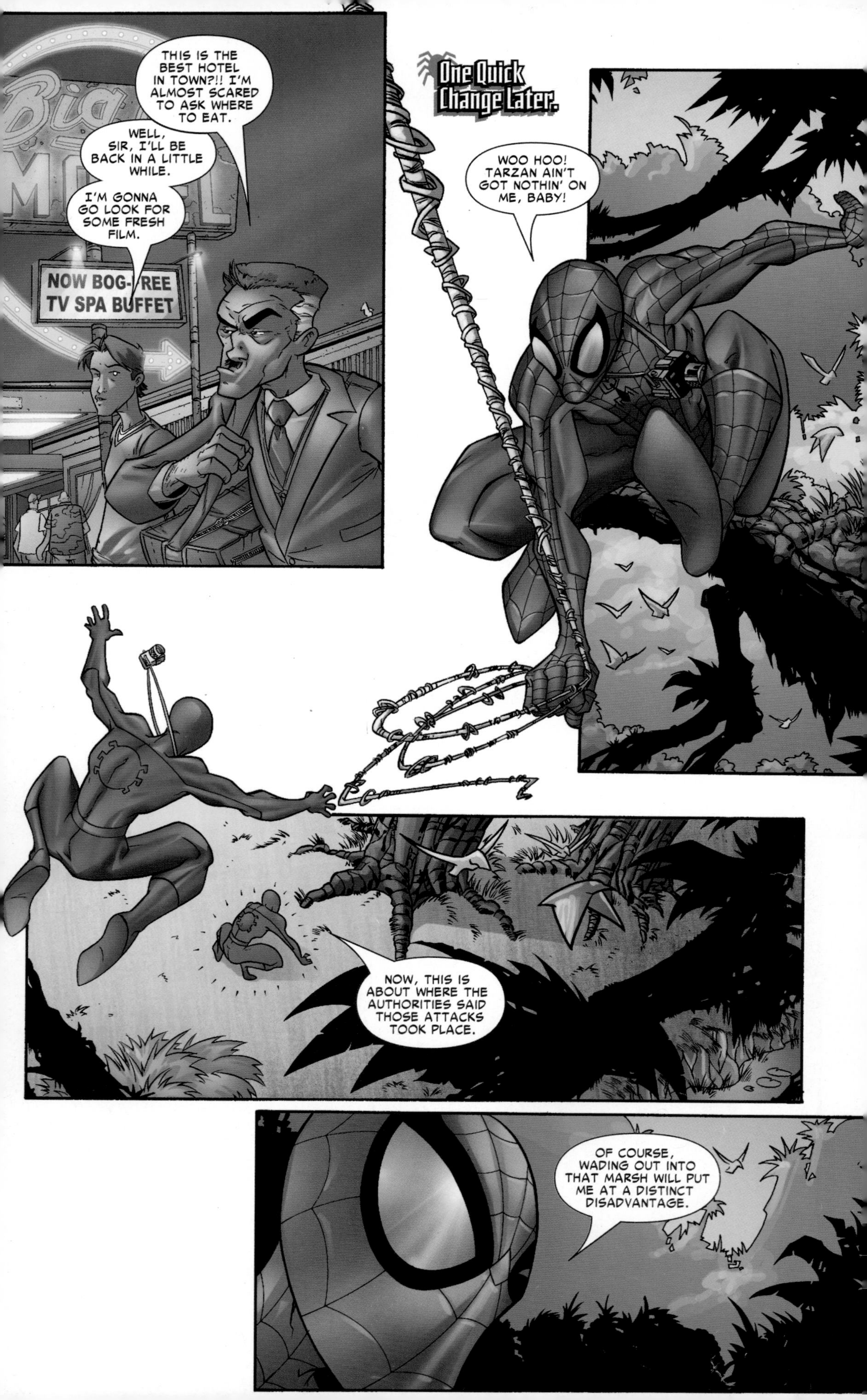
Big ... MOTEL
NOW BOG-FREE
TV SPA BUFFET
THIS IS THE BEST HOTEL IN TOWN?!! I'M ALMOST SCARED TO ASK WHERE TO EAT.
WELL, SIR, I'LL BE BACK IN A LITTLE WHILE.
I'M GONNA GO LOOK FOR SOME FRESH FILM.
One Quick Change Later.
WOO HOO! TARZAN AIN'T GOT NOTHIN' ON ME, BABY!
NOW, THIS IS ABOUT WHERE THE AUTHORITIES SAID THOSE ATTACKS TOOK PLACE.
OF COURSE, WADING OUT INTO THAT MARSH WILL PUT ME AT A DISTINCT DISADVANTAGE.

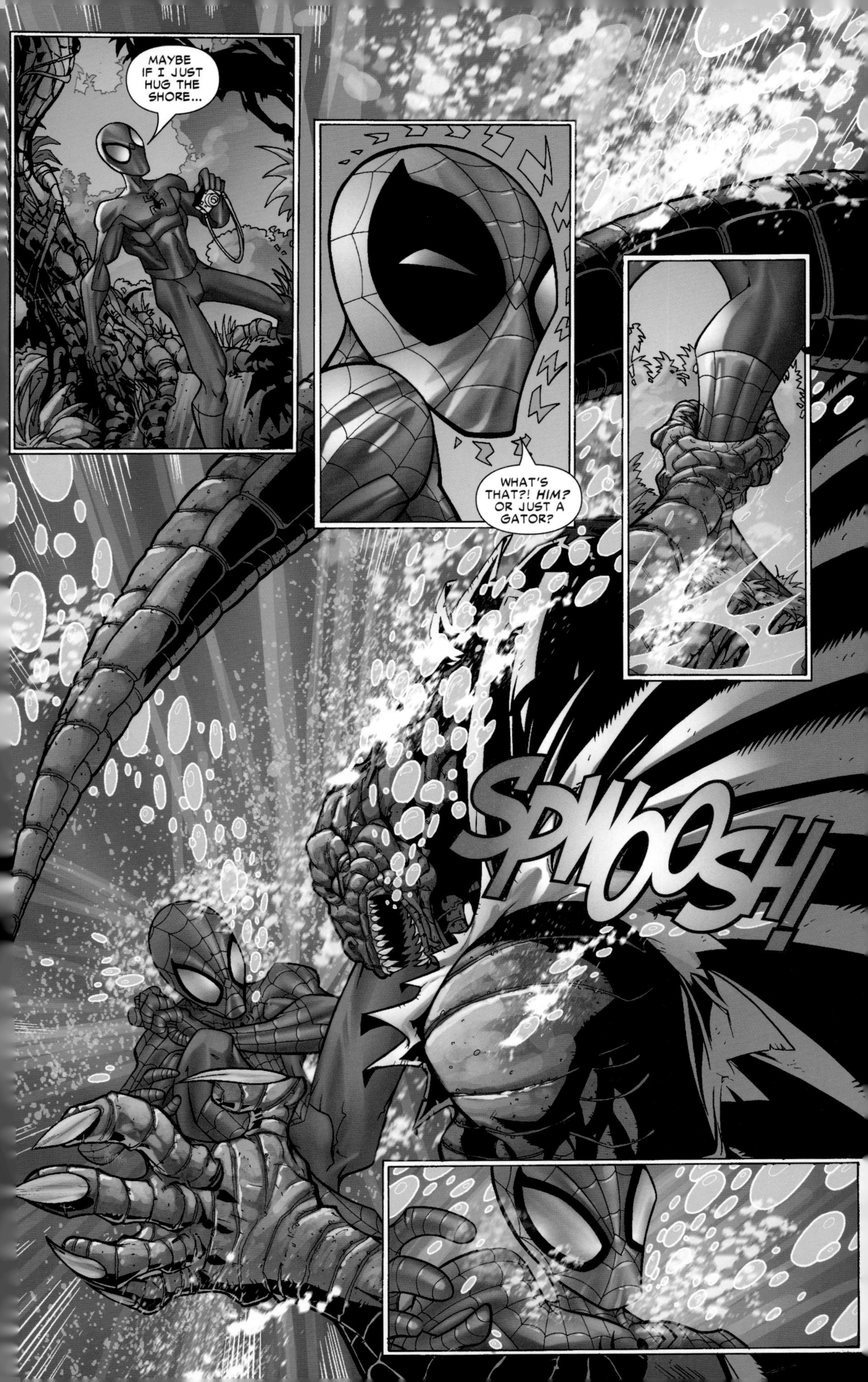

MAYBE IF I JUST HUG THE SHORE...
WHAT'S THAT?! *HIM?* OR JUST A GATOR?
SPLOOSH!

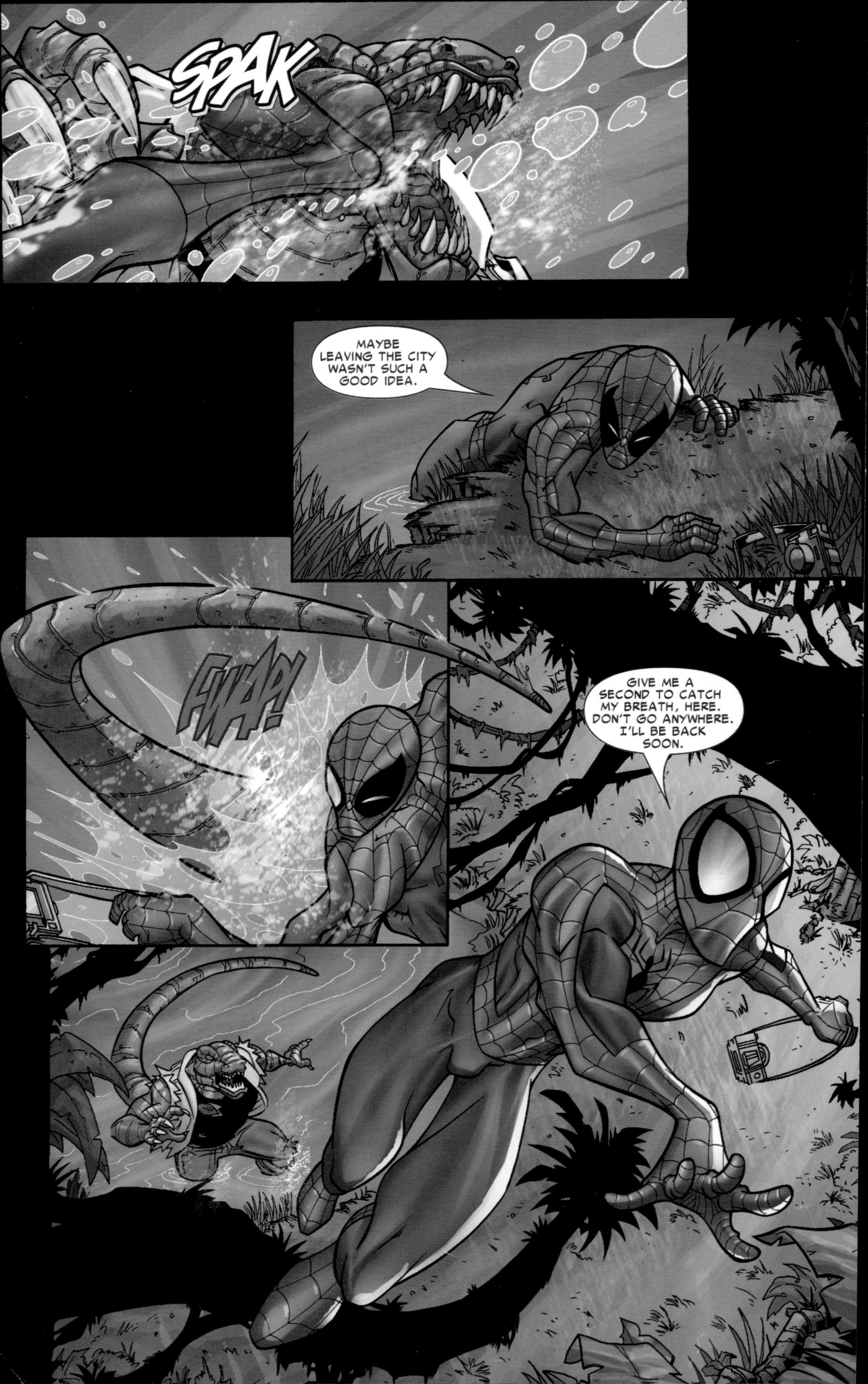
SPAK
MAYBE LEAVING THE CITY WASN'T SUCH A GOOD IDEA.
FWAP!
GIVE ME A SECOND TO CATCH MY BREATH, HERE. DON'T GO ANYWHERE. I'LL BE BACK SOON.

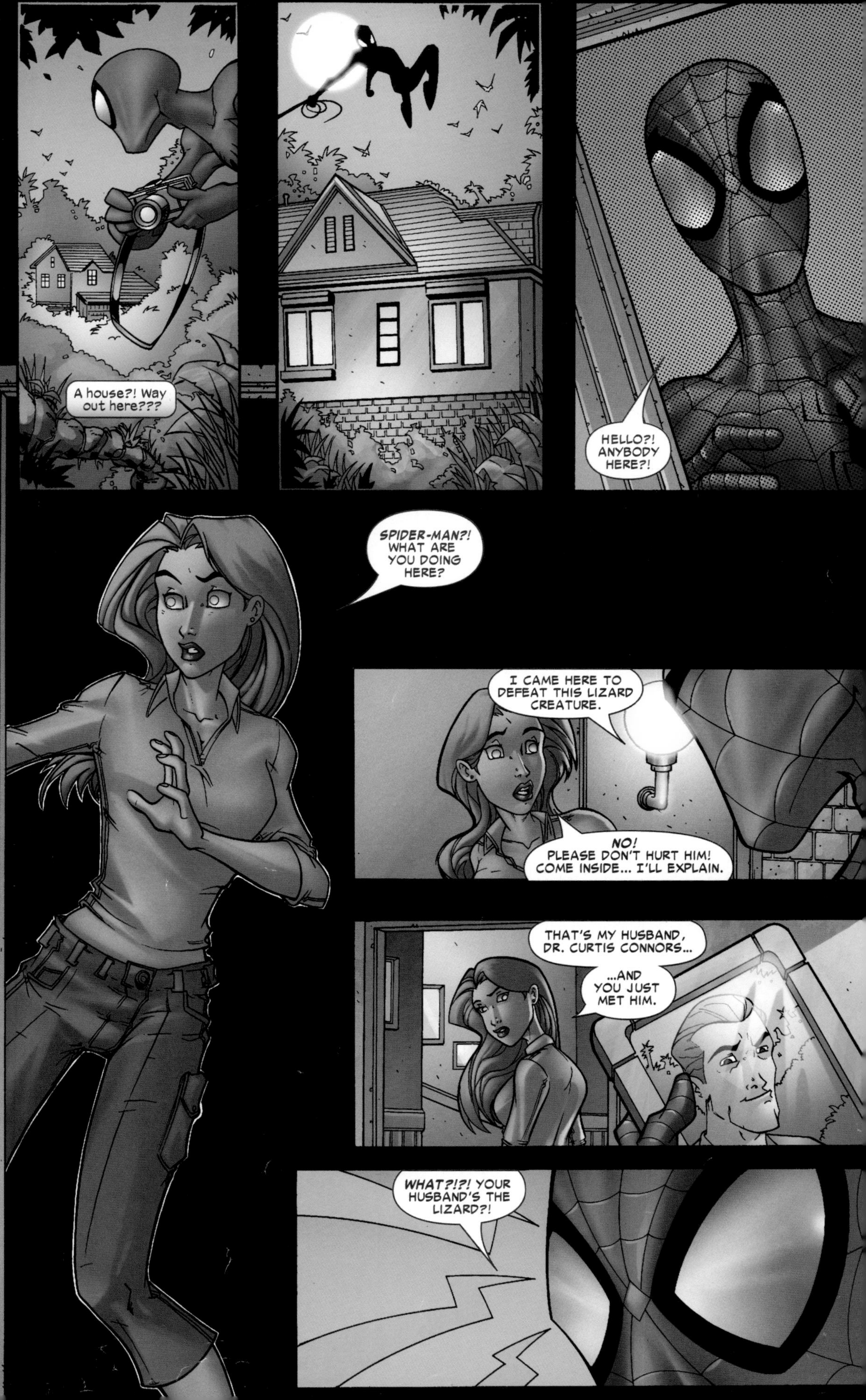
A house?! Way out here???
HELLO?! ANYBODY HERE?!
SPIDER-MAN?! WHAT ARE YOU DOING HERE?
I CAME HERE TO DEFEAT THIS LIZARD CREATURE.
NO! PLEASE DON'T HURT HIM! COME INSIDE... I'LL EXPLAIN.
THAT'S MY HUSBAND, DR. CURTIS CONNORS...
...AND YOU JUST MET HIM.
WHAT?!?! YOUR HUSBAND'S THE LIZARD?!

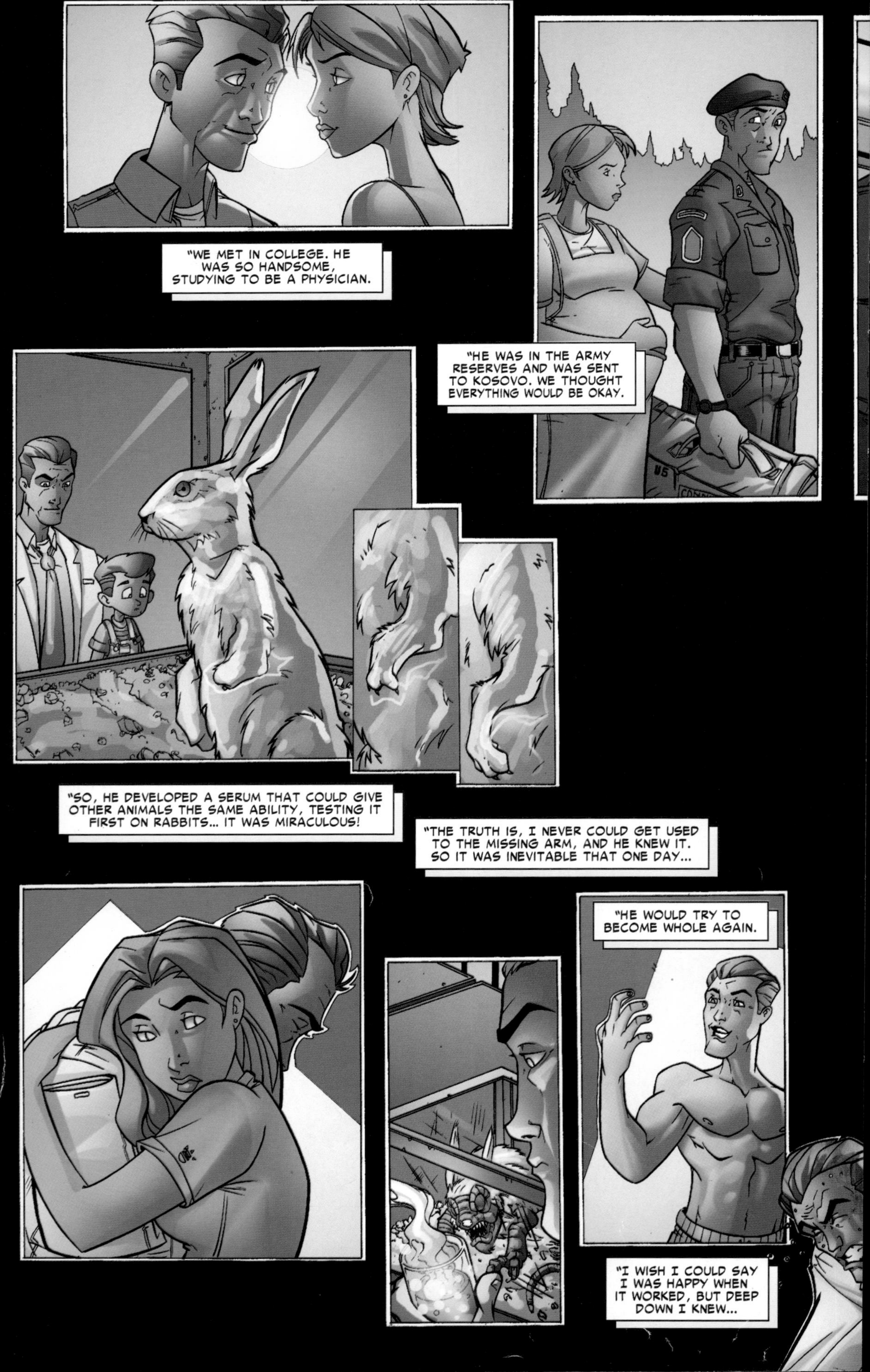
"WE MET IN COLLEGE. HE WAS SO HANDSOME, STUDYING TO BE A PHYSICIAN.
"HE WAS IN THE ARMY RESERVES AND WAS SENT TO KOSOVO. WE THOUGHT EVERYTHING WOULD BE OKAY.
"SO, HE DEVELOPED A SERUM THAT COULD GIVE OTHER ANIMALS THE SAME ABILITY, TESTING IT FIRST ON RABBITS... IT WAS MIRACULOUS!
"THE TRUTH IS, I NEVER COULD GET USED TO THE MISSING ARM, AND HE KNEW IT. SO IT WAS INEVITABLE THAT ONE DAY...
"HE WOULD TRY TO BECOME WHOLE AGAIN.
"I WISH I COULD SAY I WAS HAPPY WHEN IT WORKED, BUT DEEP DOWN I KNEW...

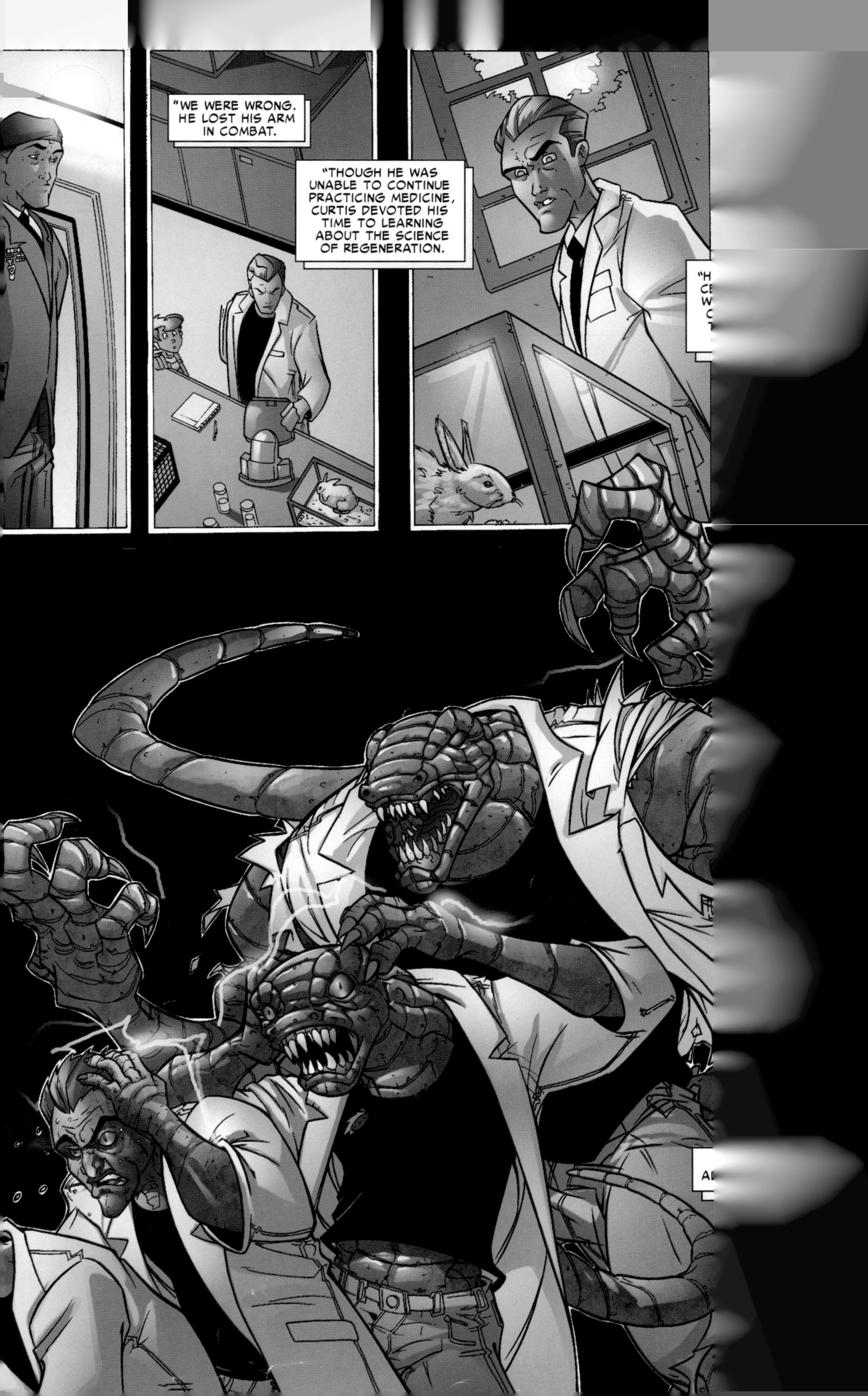
"WE WERE WRONG. HE LOST HIS ARM IN COMBAT.
"THOUGH HE WAS UNABLE TO CONTINUE PRACTICING MEDICINE, CURTIS DEVOTED HIS TIME TO LEARNING ABOUT THE SCIENCE OF REGENERATION.

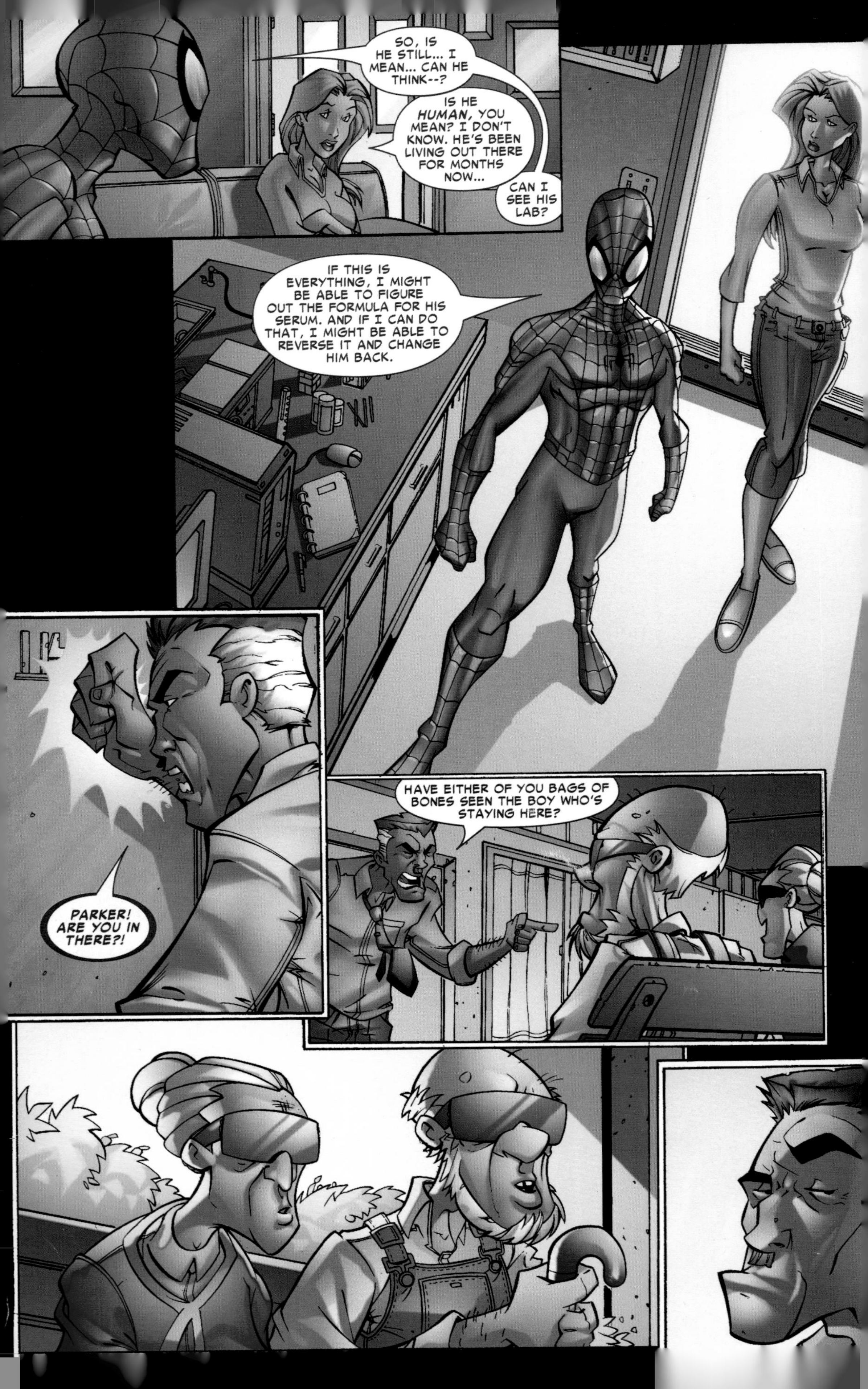
SO, IS HE STILL... I MEAN... CAN HE THINK--?
IS HE HUMAN, YOU MEAN? I DON'T KNOW. HE'S BEEN LIVING OUT THERE FOR MONTHS NOW...
CAN I SEE HIS LAB?
IF THIS IS EVERYTHING, I MIGHT BE ABLE TO FIGURE OUT THE FORMULA FOR HIS SERUM. AND IF I CAN DO THAT, I MIGHT BE ABLE TO REVERSE IT AND CHANGE HIM BACK.
PARKER! ARE YOU IN THERE?!
HAVE EITHER OF YOU BAGS OF BONES SEEN THE BOY WHO'S STAYING HERE?

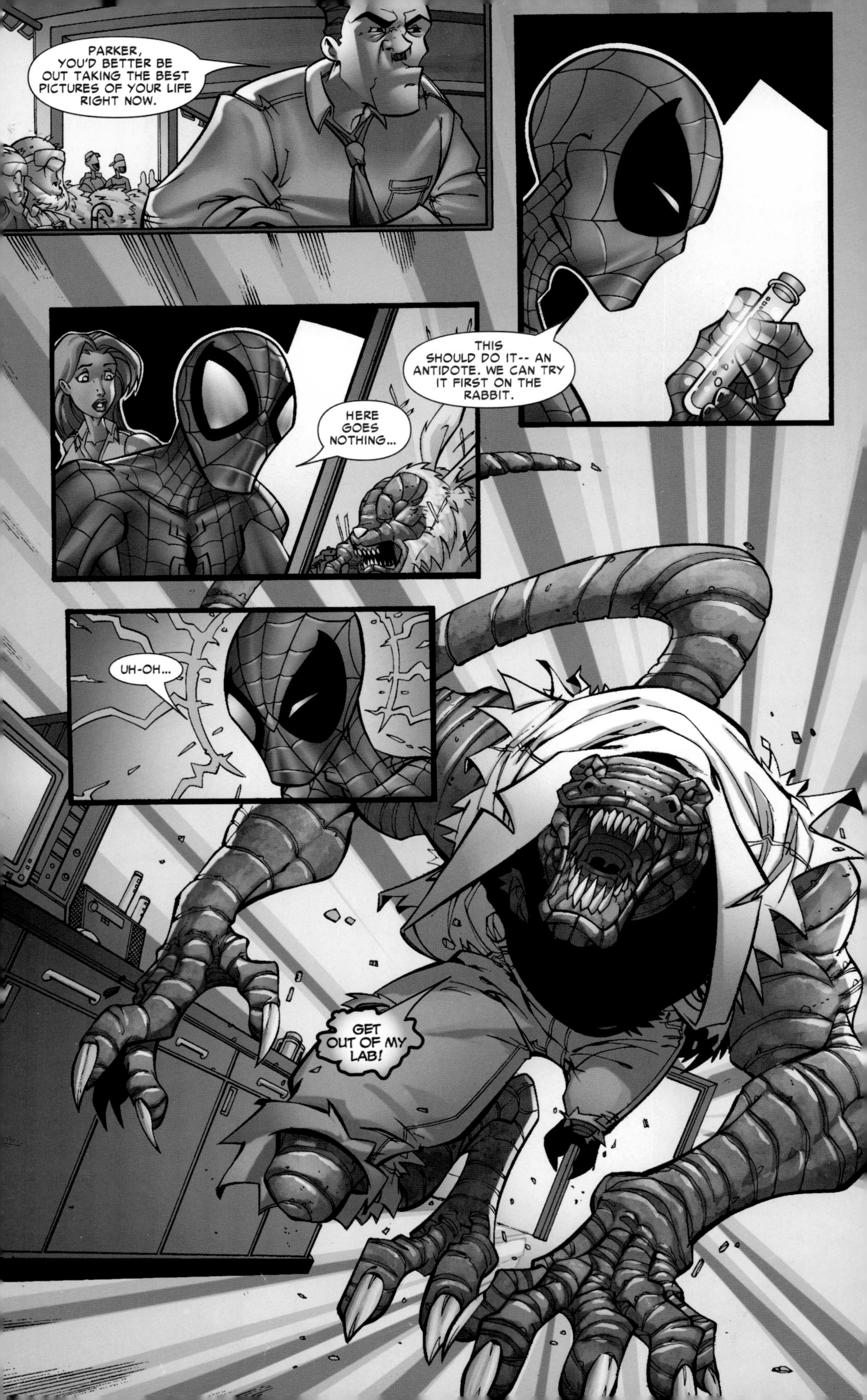
PARKER, YOU'D BETTER BE OUT TAKING THE BEST PICTURES OF YOUR LIFE RIGHT NOW.
THIS SHOULD DO IT-- AN ANTIDOTE. WE CAN TRY IT FIRST ON THE RABBIT.
HERE GOES NOTHING...
UH-OH...
GET OUT OF MY LAB!

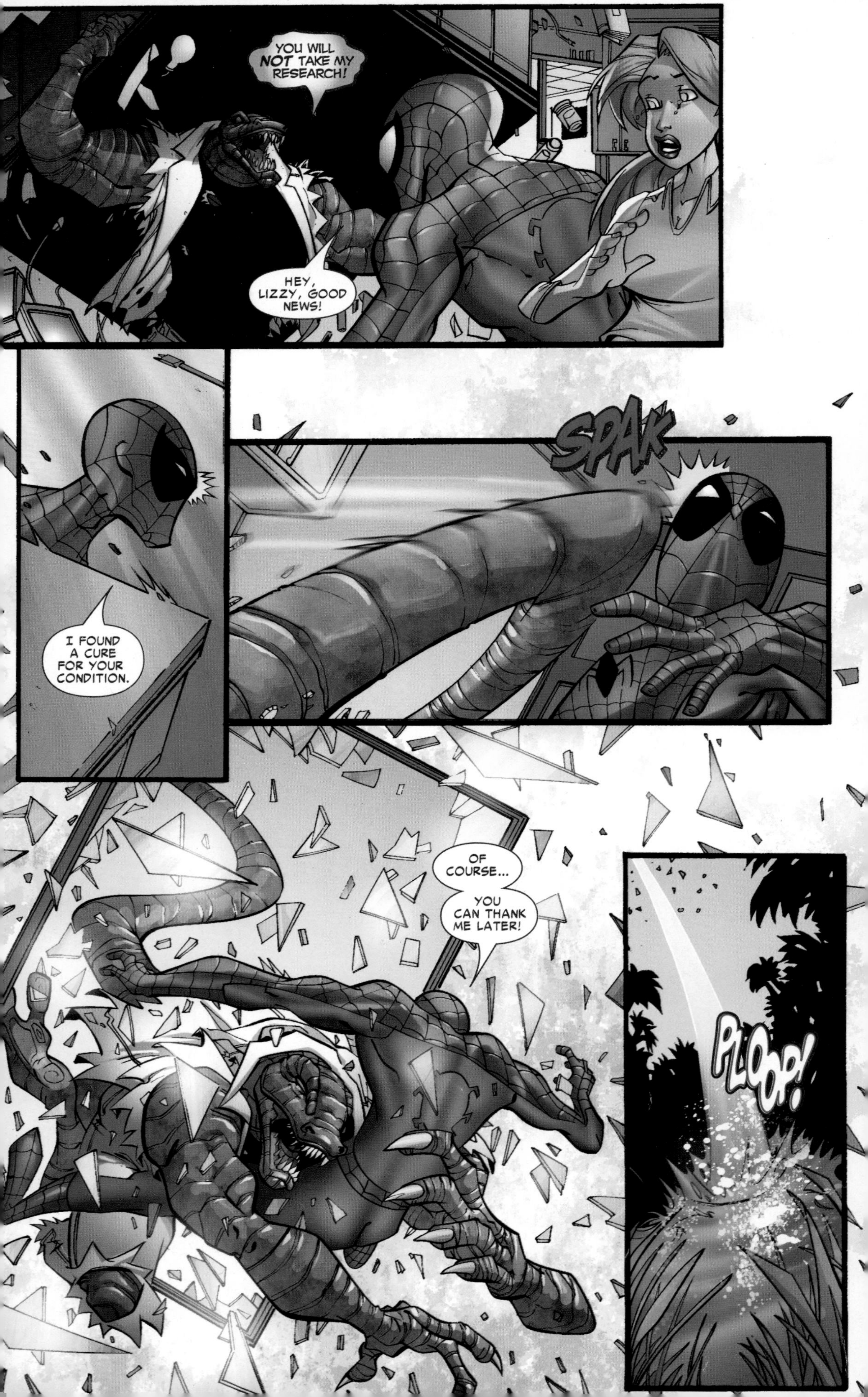
YOU WILL NOT TAKE MY RESEARCH!
HEY, LIZZY, GOOD NEWS!
I FOUND A CURE FOR YOUR CONDITION.
SPAK
OF COURSE...
YOU CAN THANK ME LATER!
PLOOP!

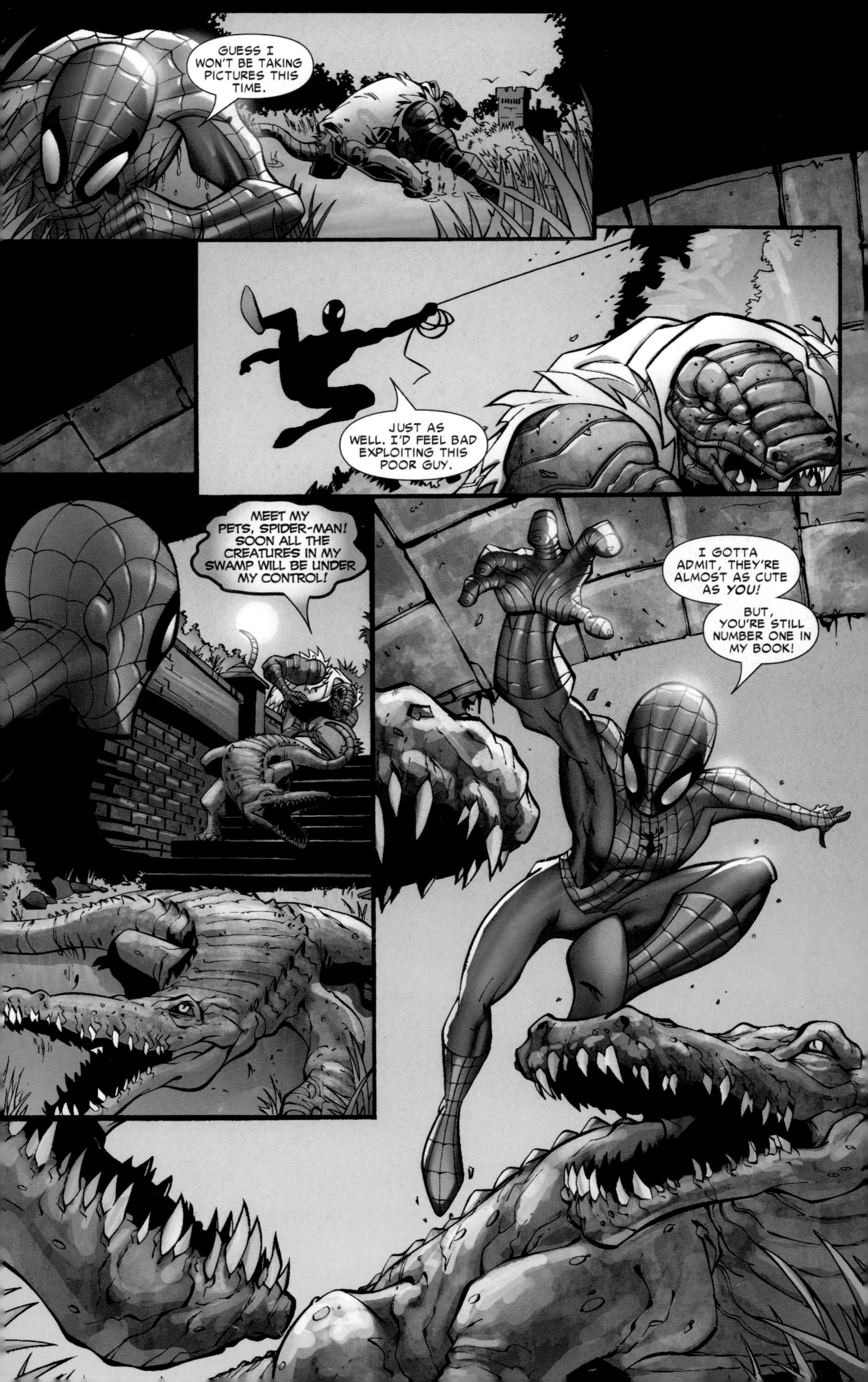
GUESS I WON'T BE TAKING PICTURES THIS TIME.
JUST AS WELL. I'D FEEL BAD EXPLOITING THIS POOR GUY.
MEET MY PETS, SPIDER-MAN! SOON ALL THE CREATURES IN MY SWAMP WILL BE UNDER MY CONTROL!
I GOTTA ADMIT, THEY'RE ALMOST AS CUTE AS YOU!
BUT, YOU'RE STILL NUMBER ONE IN MY BOOK!

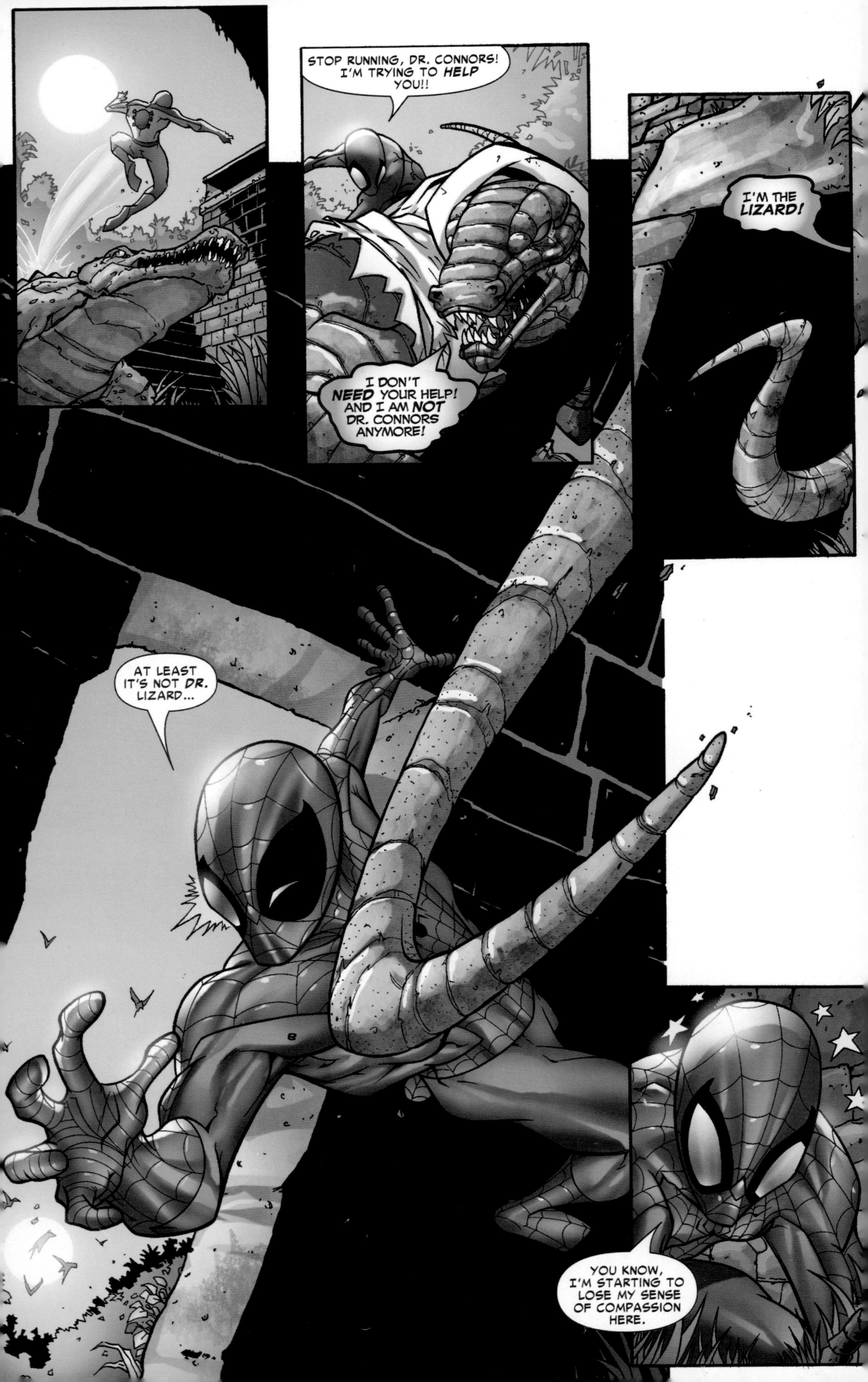
STOP RUNNING, DR. CONNORS! I'M TRYING TO HELP YOU!!
I DON'T NEED YOUR HELP! AND I AM NOT DR. CONNORS ANYMORE!
I'M THE LIZARD!
AT LEAST IT'S NOT DR. LIZARD...
YOU KNOW, I'M STARTING TO LOSE MY SENSE OF COMPASSION HERE.

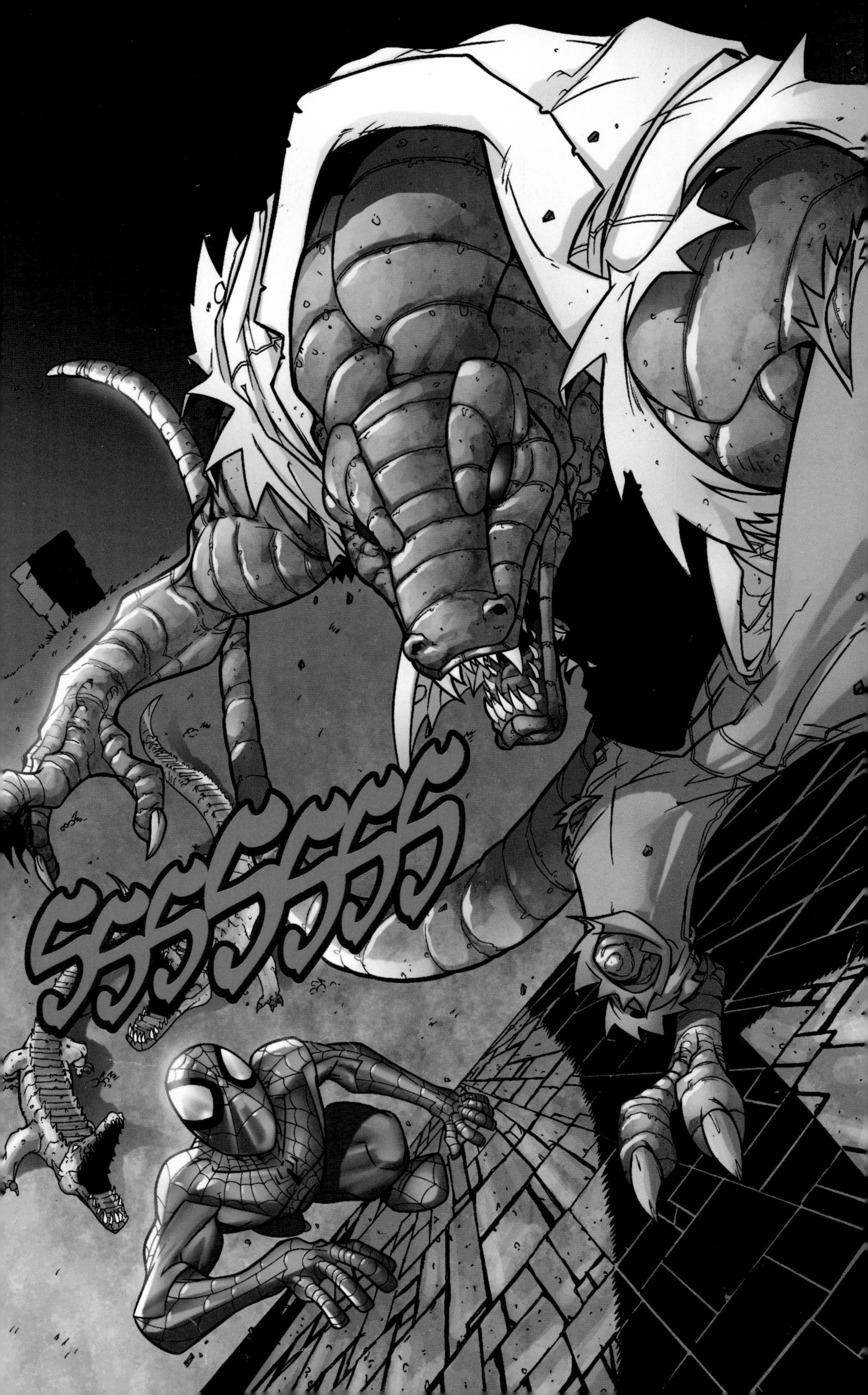
SSSSSSS

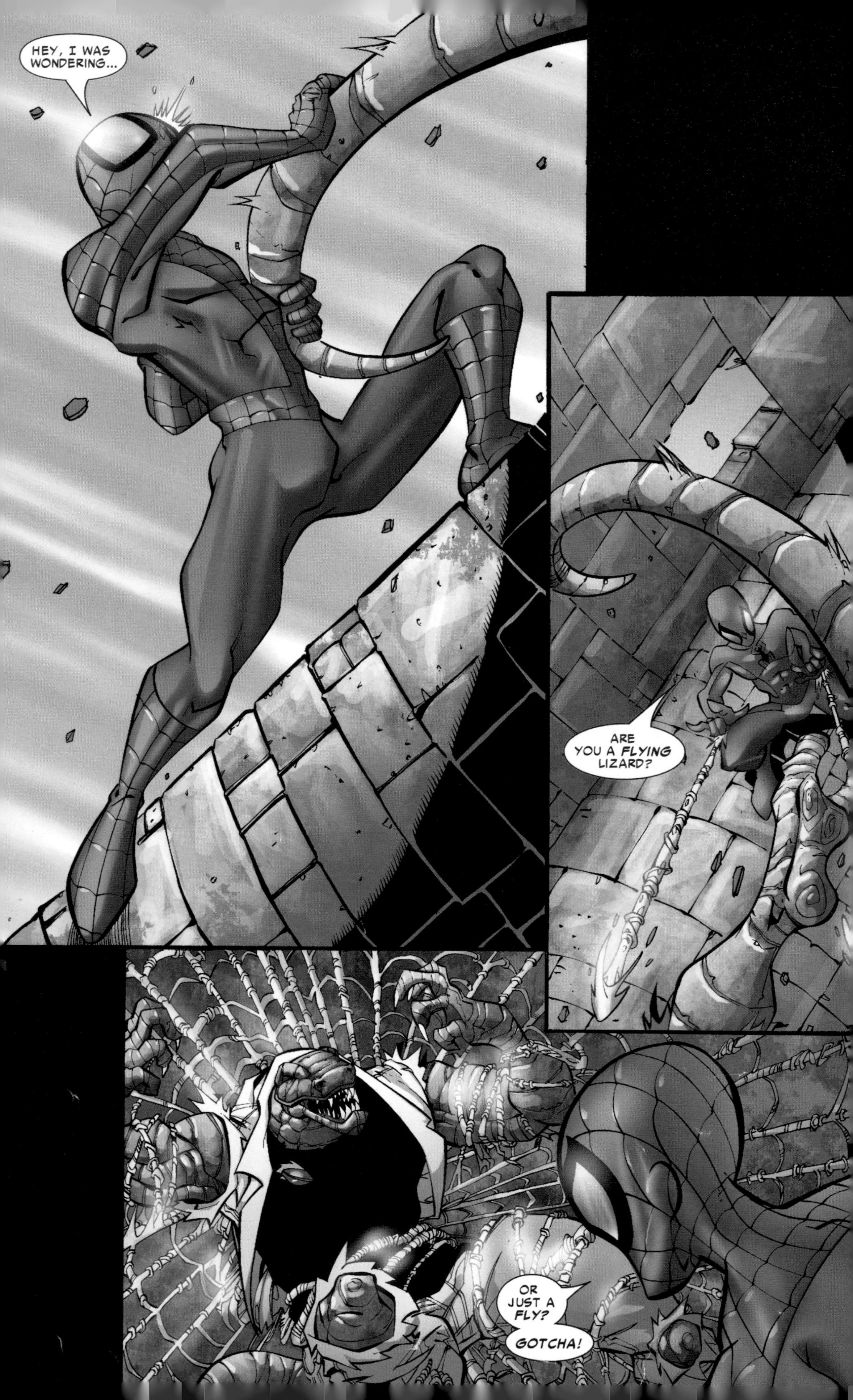
HEY, I WAS WONDERING...
ARE YOU A FLYING LIZARD?
OR JUST A FLY?
GOTCHA!

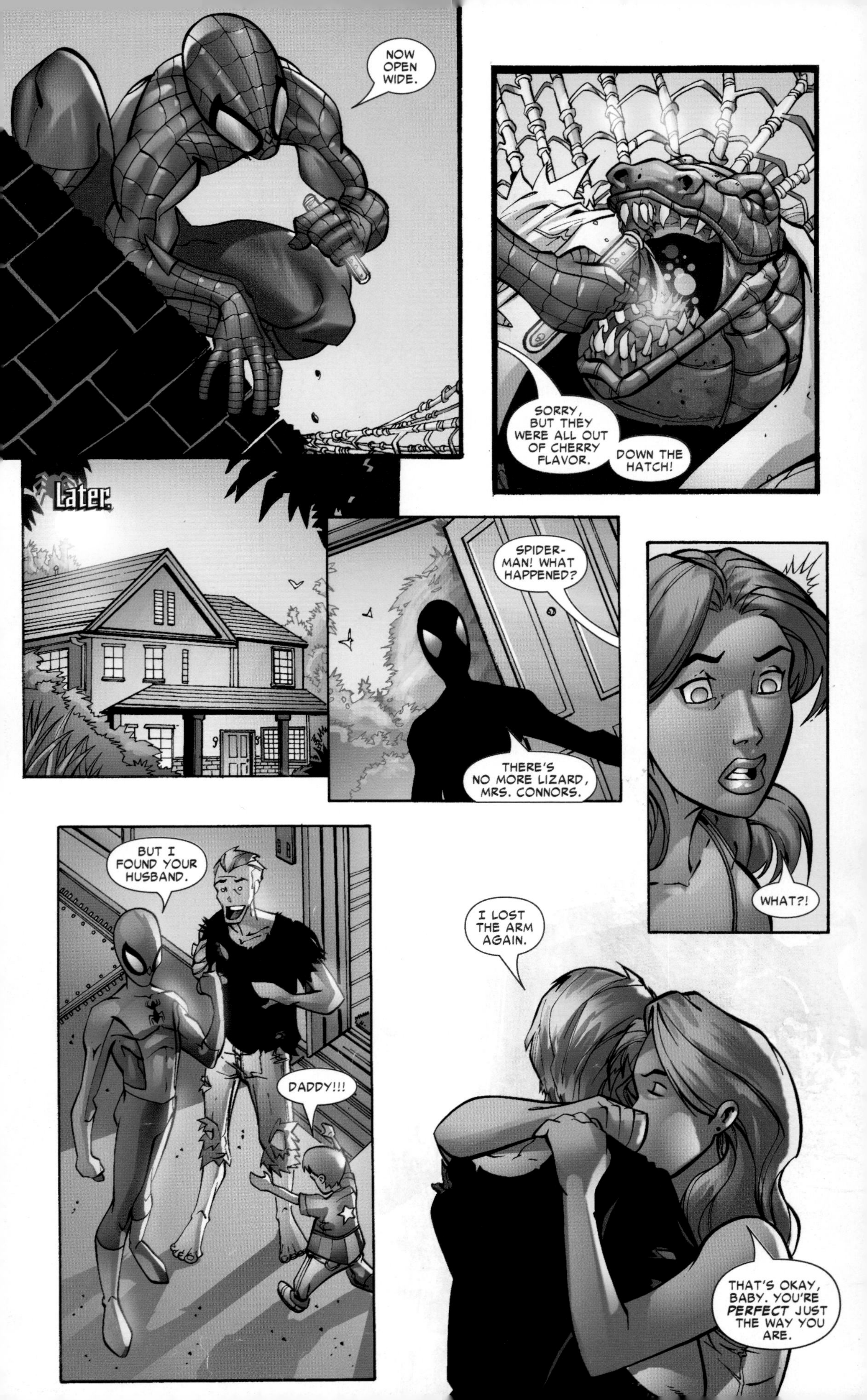
NOW OPEN WIDE.
SORRY, BUT THEY WERE ALL OUT OF CHERRY FLAVOR.
DOWN THE HATCH!
Later.
SPIDER-MAN! WHAT HAPPENED?
THERE'S NO MORE LIZARD, MRS. CONNORS.
WHAT?!
BUT I FOUND YOUR HUSBAND.
DADDY!!!
I LOST THE ARM AGAIN.
THAT'S OKAY, BABY. YOU'RE *PERFECT* JUST THE WAY YOU ARE.

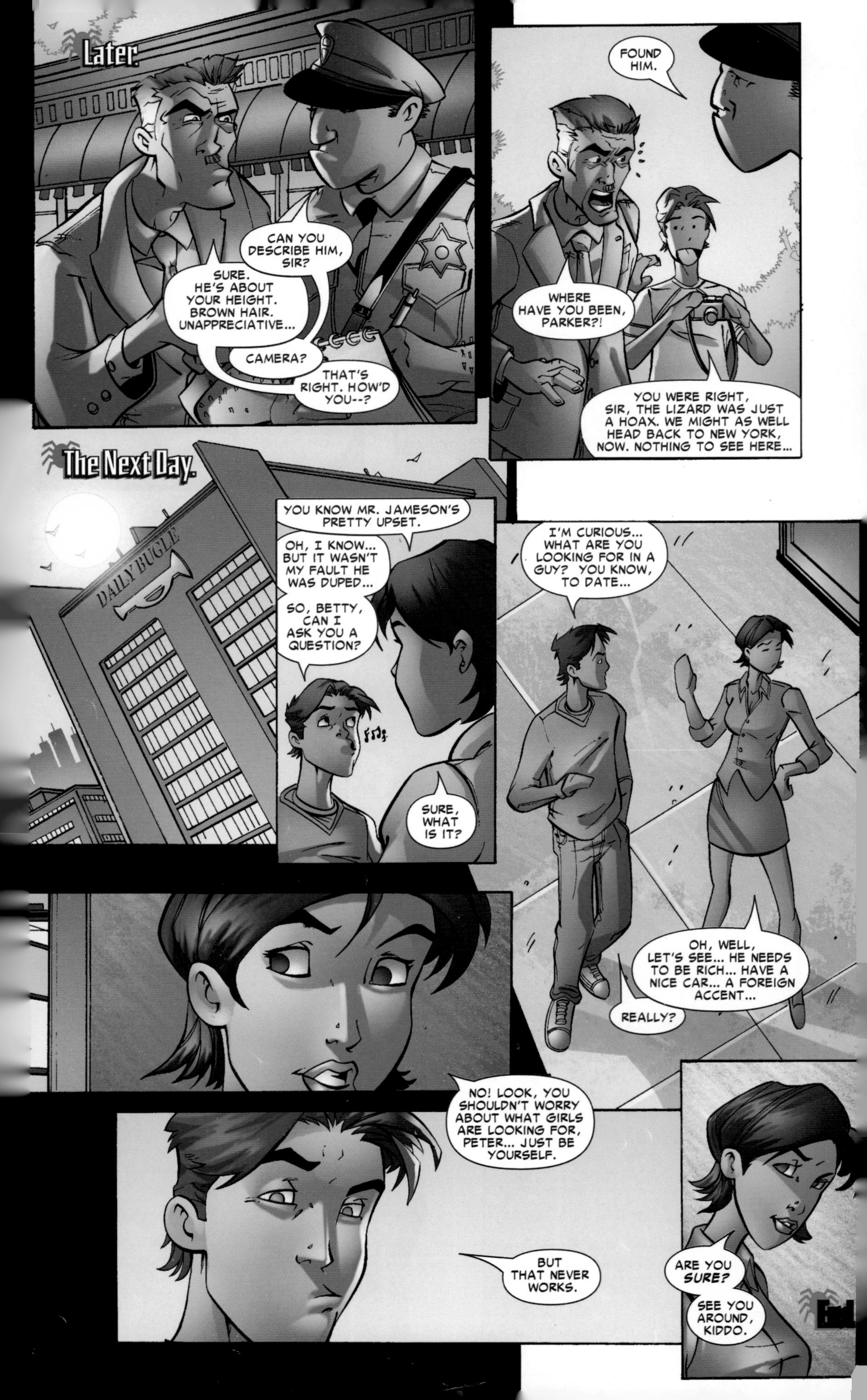
Later.
CAN YOU DESCRIBE HIM, SIR?
SURE. HE'S ABOUT YOUR HEIGHT. BROWN HAIR. UNAPPRECIATIVE...
CAMERA?
THAT'S RIGHT. HOW'D YOU--?
FOUND HIM.
WHERE HAVE YOU BEEN, PARKER?!
YOU WERE RIGHT, SIR, THE LIZARD WAS JUST A HOAX. WE MIGHT AS WELL HEAD BACK TO NEW YORK, NOW. NOTHING TO SEE HERE...
The Next Day.
DAILY BUGLE
YOU KNOW MR. JAMESON'S PRETTY UPSET.
OH, I KNOW... BUT IT WASN'T MY FAULT HE WAS DUPED...
SO, BETTY, CAN I ASK YOU A QUESTION?
SURE, WHAT IS IT?
I'M CURIOUS... WHAT ARE YOU LOOKING FOR IN A GUY? YOU KNOW, TO DATE...
OH, WELL, LET'S SEE... HE NEEDS TO BE RICH... HAVE A NICE CAR... A FOREIGN ACCENT...
REALLY?
NO! LOOK, YOU SHOULDN'T WORRY ABOUT WHAT GIRLS ARE LOOKING FOR, PETER... JUST BE YOURSELF.
BUT THAT NEVER WORKS.
ARE YOU *SURE?*
SEE YOU AROUND, KIDDO.
End